# Bill Martin Jr & Michael Sampson

**SWISH!**

Illustrated by
## Michael Chesworth

SQUARE FISH • Henry Holt and Company • New York

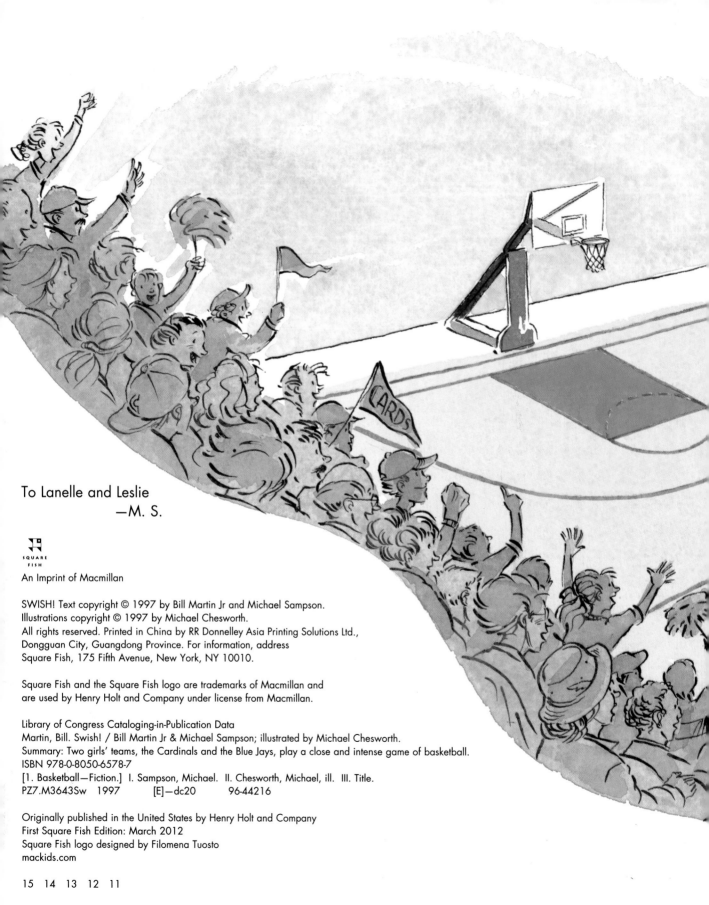

To Lanelle and Leslie
—M. S.

SQUARE
FISH

An Imprint of Macmillan

SWISH! Text copyright © 1997 by Bill Martin Jr and Michael Sampson.
Illustrations copyright © 1997 by Michael Chesworth.
All rights reserved. Printed in China by RR Donnelley Asia Printing Solutions Ltd.,
Dongguan City, Guangdong Province. For information, address
Square Fish, 175 Fifth Avenue, New York, NY 10010.

Square Fish and the Square Fish logo are trademarks of Macmillan and
are used by Henry Holt and Company under license from Macmillan.

Library of Congress Cataloging-in-Publication Data
Martin, Bill. Swish! / Bill Martin Jr & Michael Sampson; illustrated by Michael Chesworth.
Summary: Two girls' teams, the Cardinals and the Blue Jays, play a close and intense game of basketball.
ISBN 978-0-8050-6578-7
[1. Basketball—Fiction.] I. Sampson, Michael. II. Chesworth, Michael, ill. III. Title.
PZ7.M3643Sw 1997      [E]—dc20      96-44216

Originally published in the United States by Henry Holt and Company
First Square Fish Edition: March 2012
Square Fish logo designed by Filomena Tuosto
mackids.com

15  14  13  12  11

AR: 2.2 / LEXILE: AD280L

Cardinals, Blue Jays...
what a game!

The winner goes
to the hall of fame.

Less than a minute left to play,
Blue Jays have the Cards at bay.

Referee hands the ball to Lynn,
Blue Jay pass comes bouncing in.

Dribble...

dribble...

dribble...

Janet passes off to Kim,

outside shot goes off the rim.

Katie leaping
from the ground,
hustles for a high rebound.

Then down the court Katie bounds,

Dribble...

dribble...

dribble...

Jumping high into the sky,
she shoots. . .

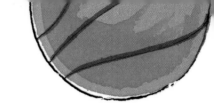

Cardinal basket!

44 to 44,
only 16 seconds more.

Blue Jays rushing,
gotta score.

Slowing now
to a coast,
Marie breaks free,
to the post.

Inside move, what a dare,
jump shot flying through the air. . .

**Blue Jay basket!**

Teams gather around the bench,
sweaty towels wiping brows.
Gotta win, the coach shows how.

One last play, and no more,
the crowd lets out a mighty roar.

Teams clasp hands and make their vows...
scoreboard makes a blaring sound.

Cardinals pass to the floor,

Dribble...

dribble...

dribble...

Like a flash,

in comes Jill,

driving hard,

tries to steal!

But Katie comes out with the ball!
The crowd goes wild!

Dribble...

dribble...

Only 3 seconds more,
pass it now, we gotta score!

Allie's open on the side.
Fake it low, but toss it high...

Dribble...

**Allie pivots on a dime,**

# throws to Cindi at the 3-point line.

Falling now,
from the sky. . .

whirling, swirling. . .

Buzzer blares, game's at end. . .
zero seconds,

# Cardinals WIN!